This Little Tiger book belongs to:

_____

_____

_____

For Mortimer

LITTLE TIGER PRESS LTD,
an imprint of the Little Tiger Group
1 Coda Studios, 189 Munster Road, London SW6 6AW
www.littletiger.co.uk
First published in Great Britain 2001
This edition published 2016
Text and illustrations copyright © Ruth Galloway 2001
Ruth Galloway has asserted her right to be identified
as the author and illustrator of this work under the
Copyright, Designs and Patents Act, 1988
A CIP catalogue record for this book
is available from the British Library
Printed in China
All rights reserved • ISBN 978-1-84869-506-1
LTP/1800/3300/0520
4 6 8 10 9 7 5

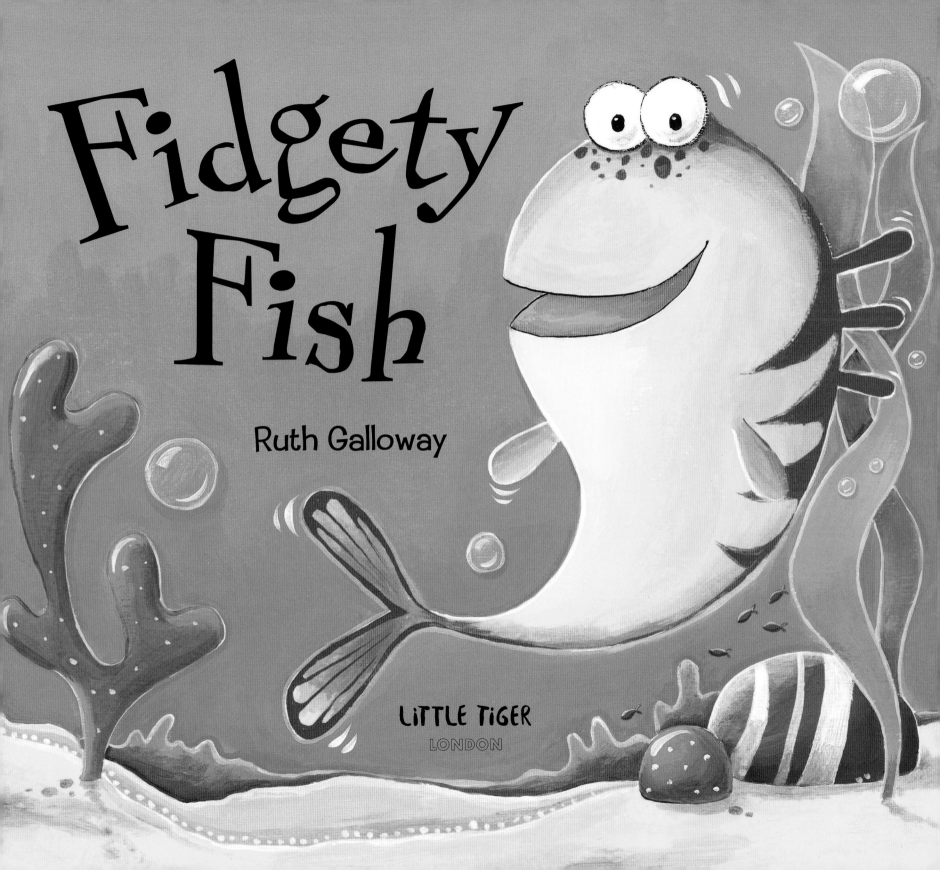

Fidgety
Fish

Ruth Galloway

LITTLE TiGER

LONDON

Tiddler was always fidgeting.

He wriggled and squiggled,

he darted and giggled . . .

until his mum got fed up with him.
"Go out into the sea and swim
till you're tired, but watch out for
the Big Fish," she said.
So Tiddler swam out of his cave.

He dived and he flipped,

he leapt and he dipped.

He sped faster than a rocket . . .

and glided gently like a swan,
letting the sea currents fan his fins.

But he still didn't feel tired!

There were limpets that clung,

and jellyfish that stung.

Tiddler swam on towards
the big, red starfish . . .

and butted it gently with his nose.
The starfish just smiled, so . . .

Tiddler asked the clickety-clackety crab to play, but it scuttled off into the seaweed.

Tiddler came to a big, dark cave.
It looked much more exciting
than his cave back home,
and Tiddler swam in . . .

Tiddler was trapped inside the Big Fish!

He trembled
and shivered,

and he shook and
he quivered . . .

until the Big Fish's tummy began to feel
very funny indeed.

It rumbled and grumbled,
it turned and it tumbled.
It fluttered and groaned,
and mumbled and moaned.

Suddenly the Big Fish
did an enormous . . .

out shot Tiddler . . .

past the jellyfish,

and the clickety-clackety
crab hiding in the weeds,

past the starfish . . .

and straight through his own
front door!

"I hope you've used up all that
energy," said his mum . . .

but she would have to wait
until the morning to hear
about his adventures,
because Tiddler
was already
fast asleep!